The Princess and the Pea

retold by Carol Ottolenghi   illustrated by Joan Clapsadle

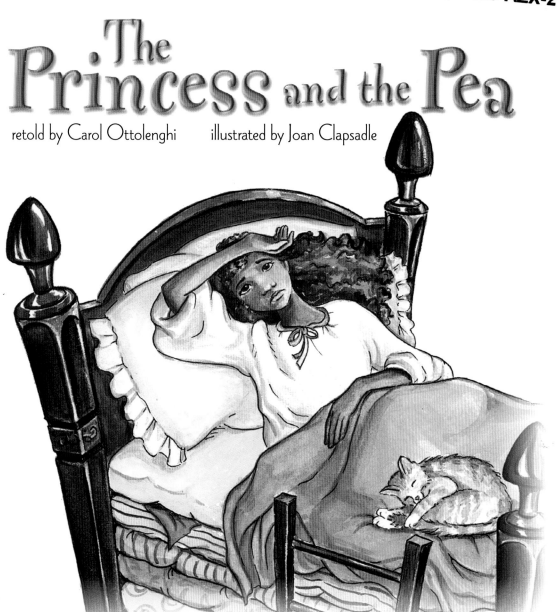

Copyright © 2009 School Specialty Publishing. Published by Brighter Child®, an imprint of School Specialty Publishing, a member of the School Specialty Family. Send all inquiries to: School Specialty Publishing, 8720 Orion Place, Columbus, Ohio 43240-2111.
Made in the U.S.A.   ISBN 0-7696-5869-5   1 2 3 4 5 6 7 8 9 10 TK 12 11 10 09 08

Long, long ago,
in a castle on a hill…

...lived a prince who was very sad. He wanted a wife and children. But he had never met a princess to marry. Not a REAL princess.

Many women came to visit the royal palace. But none of them were real princesses.

"Your wife will help rule our kingdom," the queen said. "So, she must be sensitive and caring and brave enough to help care for the citizens of our country. She must be a real princess."

One night, when the wind was howling and the rain was beating against the castle windows, there was a loud knock at the door.

When the prince opened the door, he saw a princess. At least, she said she was a princess. But was she really sensitive and caring and brave?

"It's very cold outside," said the prince, "and you are wet. Come inside and sit by the fire. I will get you some warm food to eat."

"Why were you out in the storm, Princess?" asked the queen. "Where is your horse?"

"I took some food to my sick aunt," said the princess. "On the way home, a lightning bolt struck the ground and scared my horse. He threw me and ran away."

Hum, thought the queen. *She is caring and brave. But is she sensitive? I will put a pea under her mattresses to find out.*

The queen slid the pea under
not one, not two, not three, but
twenty mattresses.

"If she feels that," the queen
said to herself, "then I will know
she is a real princess."

Soon, it was time for bed. The queen walked upstairs with the princess.

"Good night," said the queen. "I hope the storm doesn't keep you awake."

"I'm sure I'll sleep well," said the princess. "Thank you so much for letting me stay in your castle."

The princess climbed a tall
ladder to reach the top of
the bed.

"Will you be comfortable?"
asked the queen.

"Oh, yes," the princess
answered. "It is perfect."

But it wasn't perfect. The princess twisted in the bed. She turned in the bed. She even lay upside down in the bed. But she could not get comfortable.

The next morning, the princess tried to hide her giant yawns. But the queen saw her yawning.

The queen frowned at the princess. "Didn't you sleep well?" she asked the princess.

"No," said the princess. "There was something hard and lumpy in my bed."

The queen smiled. "You are a real princess!" she said.

A few months later, the prince and the princess were married. Together, they took good care of the citizens of their country.

The End.